Hiawyn Oram graduated in English and Drama and worked as a copywriter before she began to write for children in 1979. Since then she has written more than 40 children's books. Her previous titles include *Angry Arthur* (Andersen Press), and *Just Like Us* and *Billy and the Babysitter* (Orchard Books). Her first book for Frances Lincoln, *Mine!*, was illustrated by Mary Rees. She has also collaborated with the composer, Carl Davis, on two musicals for children.
Hiawyn Oram has two sons and lives in Wandsworth, London.

Mary Rees studied at Glasgow School of Art. She is a highly regarded illustrator, whose previous books include the bestseller *Ten in a Bed*, *What on Earth?* and *So What Do You Want to Be?* (Andersen Press), *Spooky Poems* (Heinemann), and *Little Pig's Tale* (Walker).
Mine!, with Hiawyn Oram, was Mary's first book for Frances Lincoln.
Mary Rees lives in Brighton.

For my brother, Tim - *H.O.*
For Alastair - *M.R.*

Little Brother and the Cough copyright © Frances Lincoln Limited 1999
Text copyright © Hiawyn Oram 1999
Illustrations copyright © Mary Rees 1999

First published in Great Britain in 1999 by
Frances Lincoln Limited, 4 Torriano Mews
Torriano Avenue, London NW5 2RZ

First paperback edition 2000

British Library Cataloguing in Publication Data
available on request

ISBN 0-7112-0844-1 hardback
ISBN 0-7112-0845-X paperback

Set in Sabon MT
Printed in Hong Kong

1 3 5 7 9 8 6 4 2

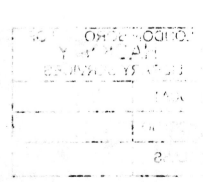

Little Brother
and the COUGH

Hiawyn Oram
Illustrated by Mary Rees

FRANCES LINCOLN

The day my mother went away and came back
with a baby, I got a cough.

"COUGH!" went the Cough.

"Come and say hello to your little brother,"
they said.

"No!" coughed the Cough. "WON'T," coughed the Cough. "COUGH! COUGH! COUGH!"

"Hush, ssh, your little brother is sleeping,"
they said.

"AND WE ARE COUGHING!" coughed the Cough.
"A BIG NOISY COUGH!"

My little brother was fed at all hours.

"Come and watch your little brother being fed," they said.

"NO!" coughed the Cough. "We're watching
television now and forever."

My little brother was bathed in his own bath with
his own soap and his own shampoo, even though
he hardly had a hair on his head.
"Come and see your little brother splashing," they said.

"WHY?" went the Cough. "We know what splashing is. SPLASHING IS SPLASHING!"

My little brother was given rattles and
cuddly toys and a musical rolling ball.

"NAAAUGH!" coughed the Cough.
"WE WANT RATTLES AND CUDDLY TOYS
AND A BABY'S ROLLING BALL!"

My little brother smiled his first smile and everyone
in the neighbourhood was called in to see.
"Isn't this great? Isn't this sweet?" they cooed.
"Your little brother can smile!"

"AND WE CAN STAND ON OUR HEAD,"
coughed the Cough.

My little brother was put in his pram under the tree.

"Let's creep up to him," coughed the Cough.

"No one is watching. Let's rock his pram . . .

AND ROCK HIS PRAM AND ROCK HIS PRAM
AND ROCK HIS PRAM UNTIL IT TIPS OVER
AND TIPS HIM OUT!" coughed the Cough . . .

And this time everybody heard and came running.

"What a Bad Cough you have!" they cried.

"What a very Bad Cough. What a very very VERY
Bad Cough . . ."

And they put us to bed and gave us hot drinks
and hot water bottles and a cuddly bear and
some colouring books and a musical box with
a ballerina inside . . .

and sat on the bed and soothed us and read
to us and coloured in with us until the Cough
decided it had no more to do in our house and
crept away in the night . . .

and I could get up and say, "Hello,
Little Brother . . . This is a musical box.
And I am your Big Sister . . ."

and watch him . . .

watch him . . .

SMILE!

MORE PICTURE BOOKS IN PAPERBACK
FROM FRANCES LINCOLN

MINE!
Hiawyn Oram
Illustrated by Mary Rees

Isabel went to play with Claudia. She climbed onto Claudia's rocking horse. "Mine!" shrieked Claudia and pushed her off. Poor Isabel has a hard time, trying to play with her friend. But in the end it is Isabel who gets the last laugh. A witty and original picture book for the very young.

Suitable for National Curriculum English - Reading, Key Stage 1
Scottish Guidelines English Language - Reading, Level A

ISBN 0-7112-0682-1 **£4.99**

ELEPHANTS DON'T DO BALLET
Penny McKinlay
Illustrated by Graham Percy

When Esmeralda the elephant wants to be a ballerina, Mummy's not so sure – after all, elephants don't do ballet. But Esmeralda joins a ballet class. She gets her trunk in a tangle, but goes on triumphantly to prove that elephants *can* do ballet!

Suitable for National Curriculum English - Reading, Key Stage 1
Scottish Guidelines English Language - Reading, Level A

ISBN 0-7112-1130-2 **£4.99**

CINDERELLA AND THE HOT AIR BALLOON
Ann Jungman
Illustrated by Russell Ayto

Go to the boring old ball? Cinderella would far rather throw her own party! A hilarious new version of the well-known fairy story that every child will love.

Suitable for National Curriculum English - Reading, Key Stages 1 and 2
Scottish Guidelines English Language - Reading, Level B

ISBN 0-7112-1051-9 **£4.99**

Frances Lincoln titles are available from all good bookshops.
Prices are correct at time of publication but may be subject to change.